GW01005518

You can't do that!

Sue Wood

Funky Gerbil Press

First published in 2014 in England by

Funky Gerbil Press

Words and illustrations Copyright © 2014 Sue Wood

www.funkygerbil.com
hello@funkygerbil.com

Funky Gerbil Press is an imprint of

Explainer HQ Ltd
Fifth Floor
Horton House
Exchange Flags
Liverpool
L2 3PF
England

www.explainerhq.com

This title is available directly from all good retailers. Bulk
discount available for educational institutions through Funky
Gerbil Press.

British Library Cataloguing in Publication Data.
A catalogue record for this book is available from the British
Library.

ISBN 978-1-909320-61-1

All rights reserved by the publisher.

For Rachael and Lucy

An elephant wanted to walk through the sky ...

He looked past the wire
and he let out a sigh ...

The earth seemed so far away, distant and pale
and doubts whispered in as he looked down the dale.
'You can't do that,' said a voice in his head,
'step off and be safe, go backwards instead.'

His tummy went gurgle, and flippety flop.
His heart kept him going, his head made him stop.

4

A fireman came with a ladder and crew,
he shouted up loudly 'I know what to do.'
'It's dangerous balancing up on that wire
and in my opinion you're playing with fire!'
'Just sidle back slowly and don't get upset
or if you prefer you can jump in our net.'

His tummy went gurgle, and flippety flop.
His heart kept him going, his head made him stop.

A doctor arrived with a book to consult.
'From what I can see this is nobody's fault.'
'You think you are able to do what you can't.'
'Let's look at this all from a different slant.'

'There's so many other things that you could do,
just get yourself down and I'll tell you a few.'

His tummy went gurgle,
and flippety flop.
His heart kept him going,
his head made him stop.

7

A newspaper man came to write down the story,
the headline was 'Animal falls from Glory'.
'Let's change things a bit and say you're a horse,
it's all about you (and the tightrope of course).'
'Just come down a minute and give me your view,
let's capture this moment in time for you.'

Daily Scandal

Old woman in shoe finally ties knot

50p

wow.scandal.co.uk

Wednesday 18 June 2014

ANIMAL FALLS FROM GLORY

 Little Miss Muffet: new pet is a spider

■ Queen's men put Humpty together again

STORY BY MAY K BELIEVE

LESS THAN 2 HOURS AFTER ATTEMPTING TO WALK ACROSS A TIGHTROPE EX-OLYMPIC HORSE IS TREATED FOR SHOCK

LIBRARY PICTURE BY IVOR PHONE

Walkers gathered to watch a horse attempt to walk from the famous vantage point Dizzy Heights, across a 1.6km tightrope, to the opposite summit of Clearly Knot.

A group of professionals gathered to try to persuade him down, but the horse (Mrs Ellie Fant), said nay to those imploring her to step off the tightrope. A fireman on the scene commented that "This is a very blinkered animal." A spokesman from BITS (British Institute of Tightrope Survivors), defended Ellie by stating that "..he did not have any form of blindfold during this attempt."

CONTINUED ON PAGE 4

COMMENT 12-13 **FOOD** 14-15 **SOAPS & DETERGENTS** 28-32 **READERS' (&SCENIC) VIEWS** 43

NEWS

Fake sea shells found on seashore
PAGE 2

Mice sue over clock strike
PAGE 8

Revealed: Location of peck of pickled pepper
PAGE 17

His tummy went gurgle
and flippety flop.

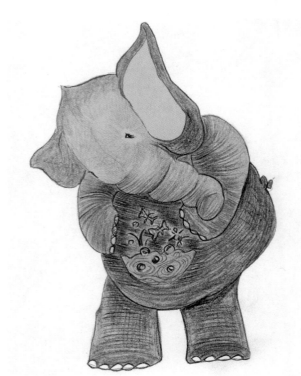

His heart kept him going ...

A little boy Ben came and noticed him there,
frozen in time way up high in the air.
He sat himself down and he marvelled aloud
at the stangeness of nature constructing a cloud
that looked like an elephant, large and grey
and all on a beautiful summer's day.

His tummy
went
gurgle

And
flippety
flop

His heart
kept him
going

His head
made him
stop.

The elephant looked at the fire crew again,
the doctor, the press and the little boy Ben.
'I'm so far away from them, what can they do?'
he took a deep breath and he visibly grew.
He straightened his back and his confidence showed,
he smiled, he relaxed, you could say that he glowed.

15

He took a step forward,
he felt the taut wire.
He knew that his dreams
could not hope to be higher.

He held the pole loosely.
He balanced it right.

He'd lost all the doubt,
all that niggling fright.
With lightness not known
to the elephants' kind ...

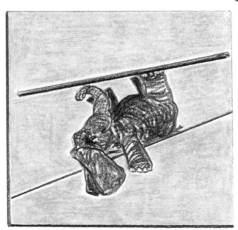

he let himself go from
the fear in his mind.

The firemen cheered.
The doctor applauded.

The man from the press
said they'd all been rewarded.
And through their support
he had ground-breaking news.
He could interview all,
he could write great reviews.

All the firemen said
'A good job well done.'
'We made the place safe
and we let him have fun.'

The doctor agreed and began her report
on managing fear in a dangerous sport.
She looked at the boy sitting still on the ground
and asked him what thoughts or concerns he had found.

The boy kept on looking and looking again.
He said that he thought it would soon start to rain.

And what of the elephant? What was he doing?
He'd finished his walk and was thoughtfully chewing
a little light lunch as he planned his next mission ...

His mind clearly set on his burning new vision
to run in a marathon right through the city ...
We've run out of pages now, oh what a pity!

6364103R20018

Printed in Great Britain
by Amazon.co.uk, Ltd.,
Marston Gate.